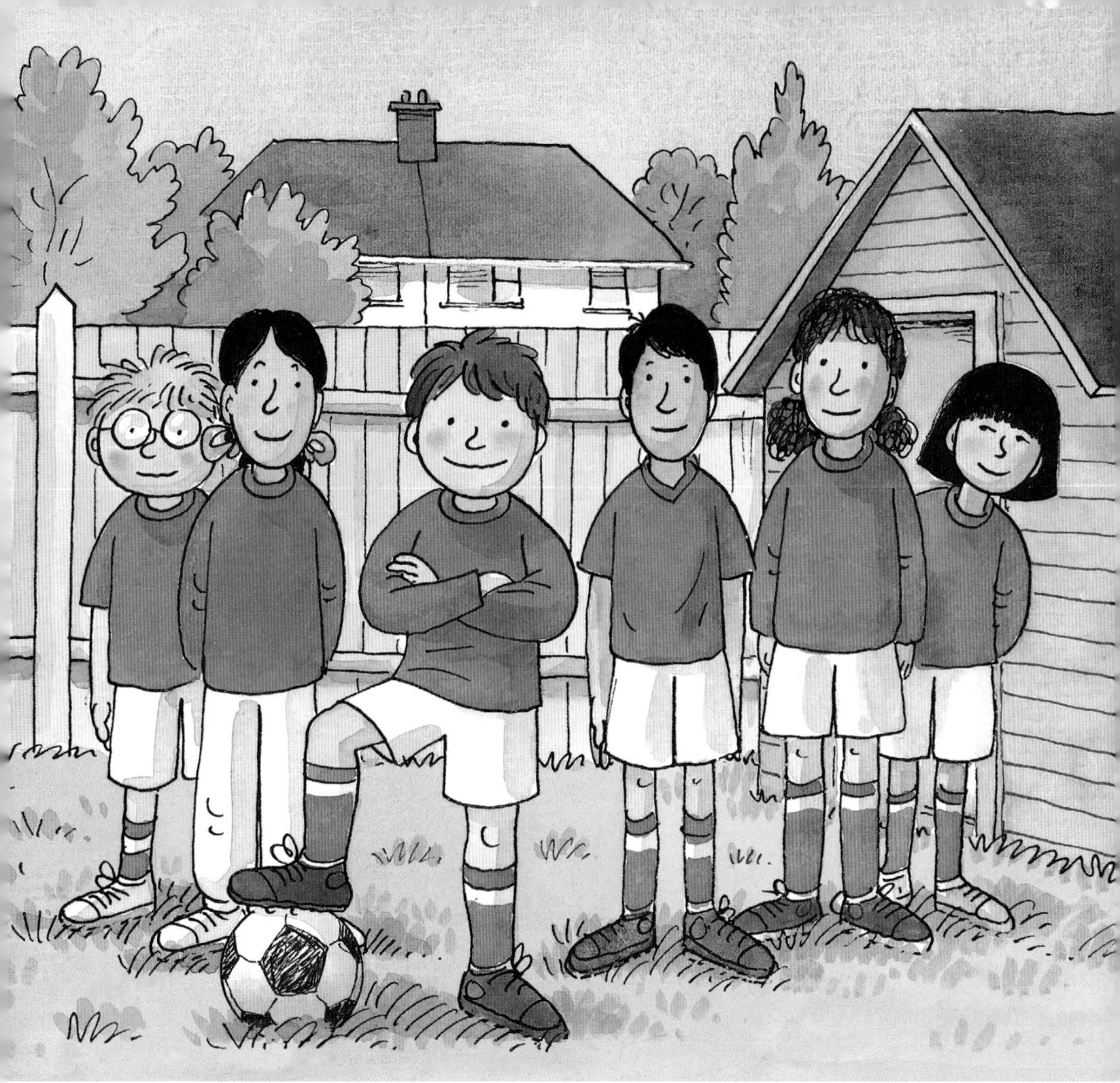

We are all in red.

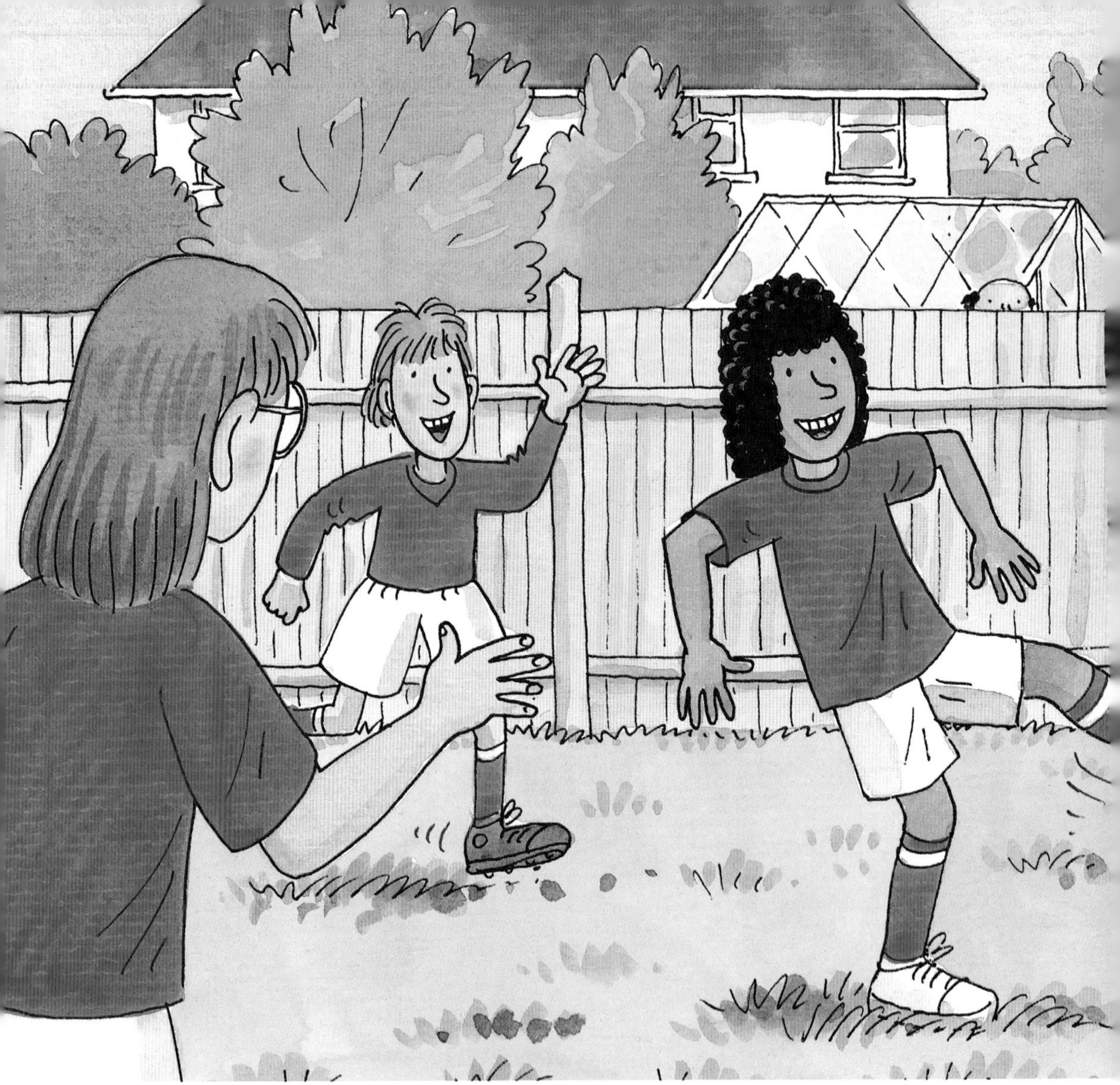

We are all in blue.

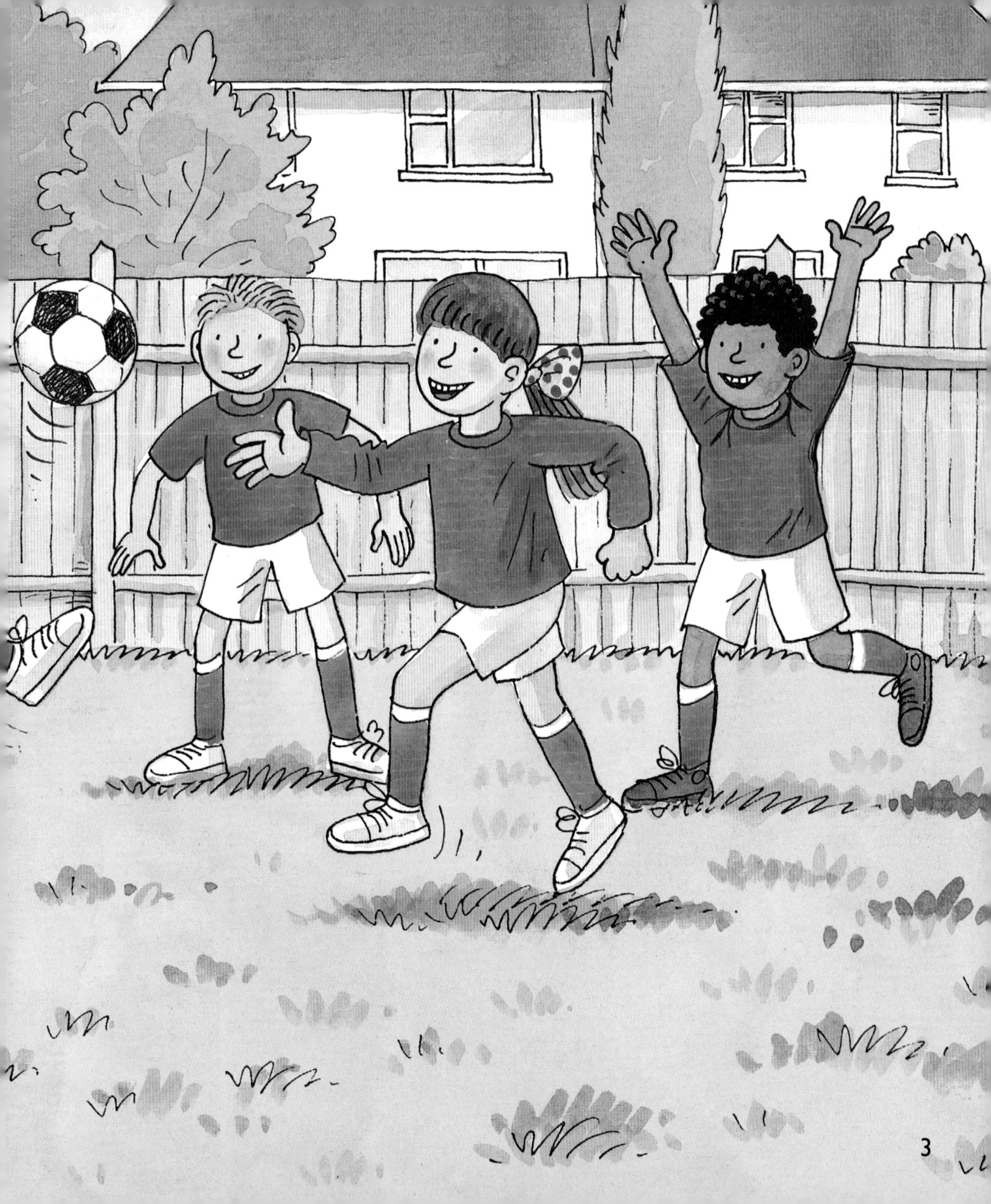

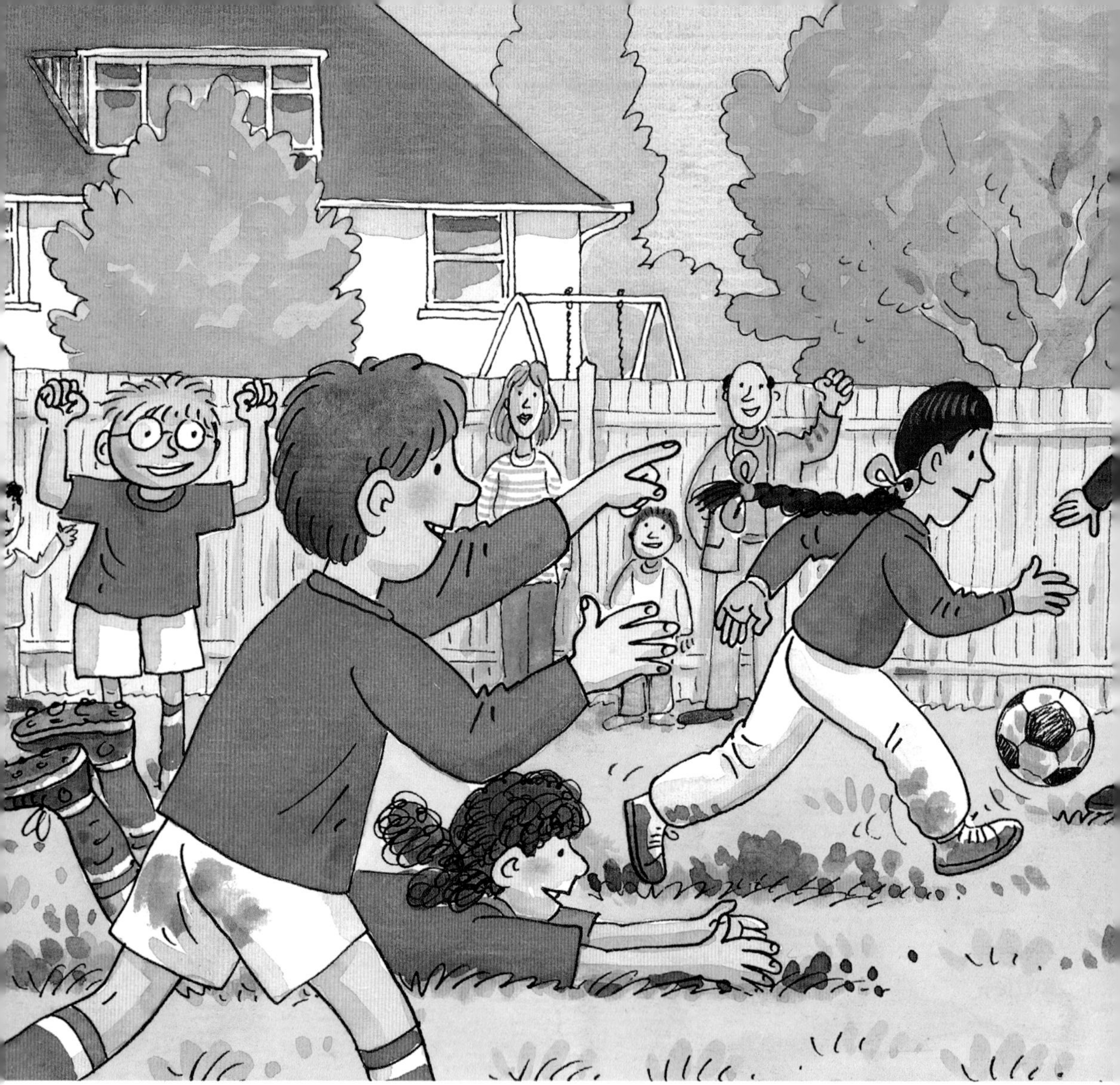

Come on the reds!

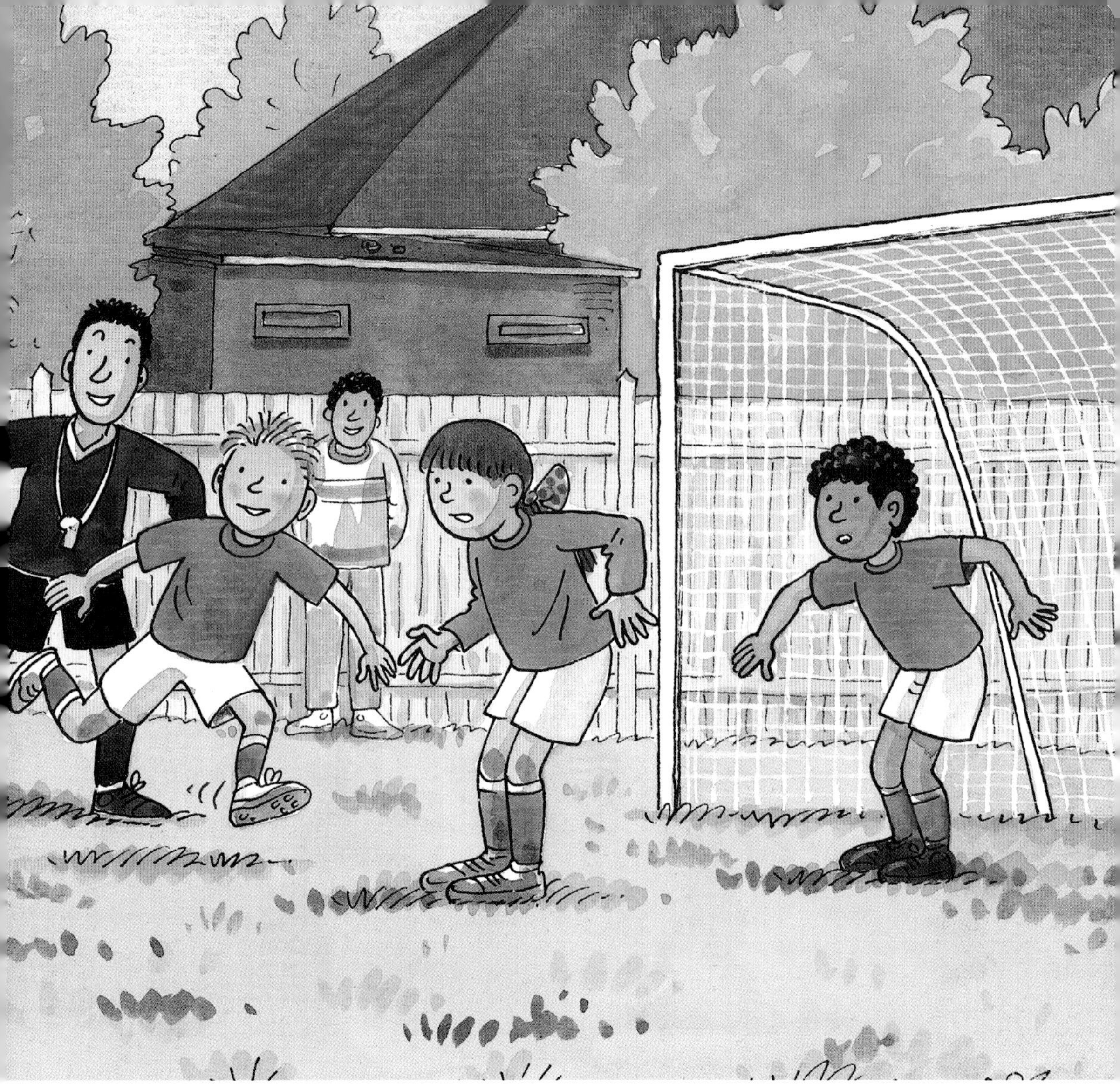

Come on the blues!

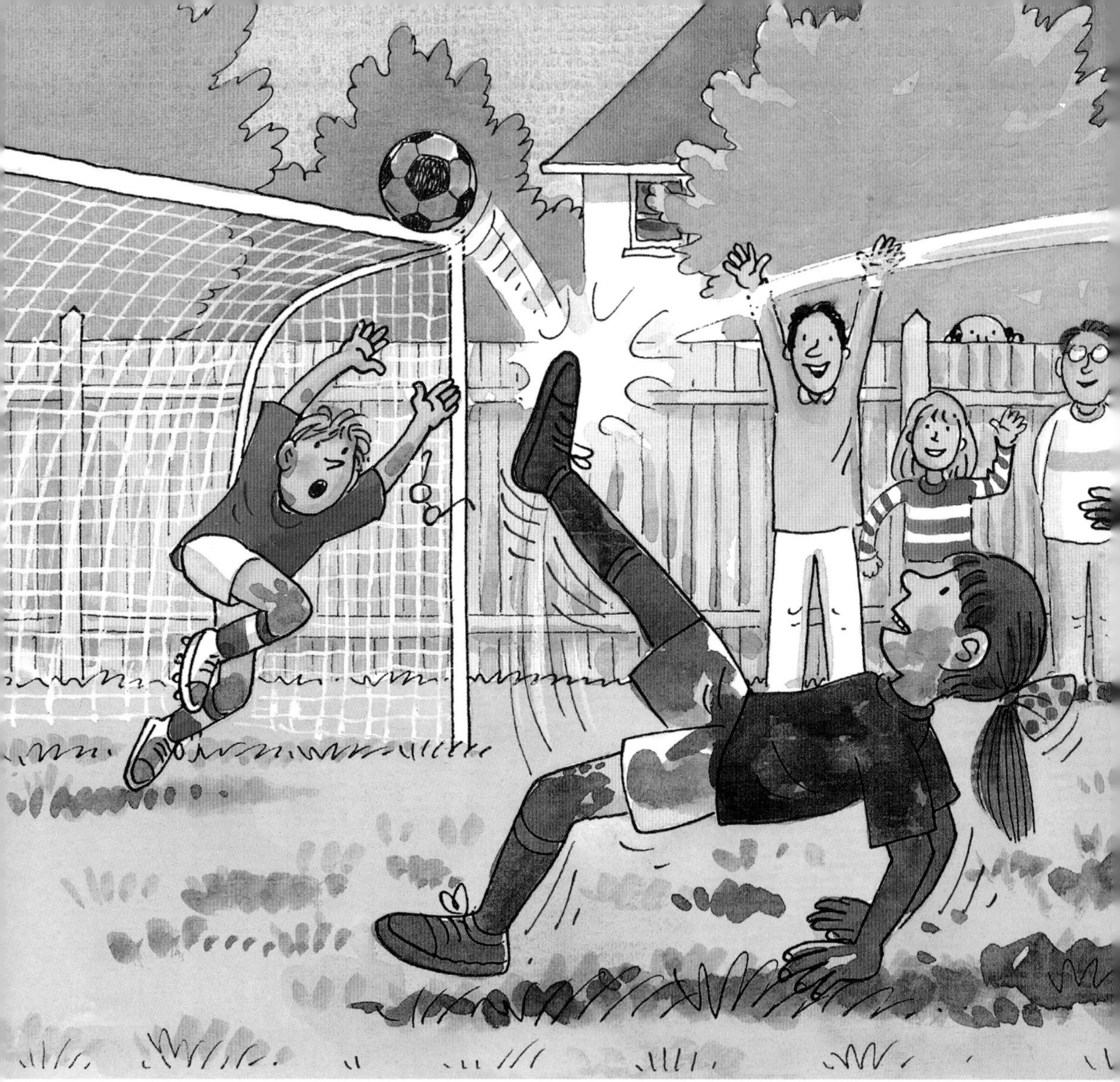

Who is in red?

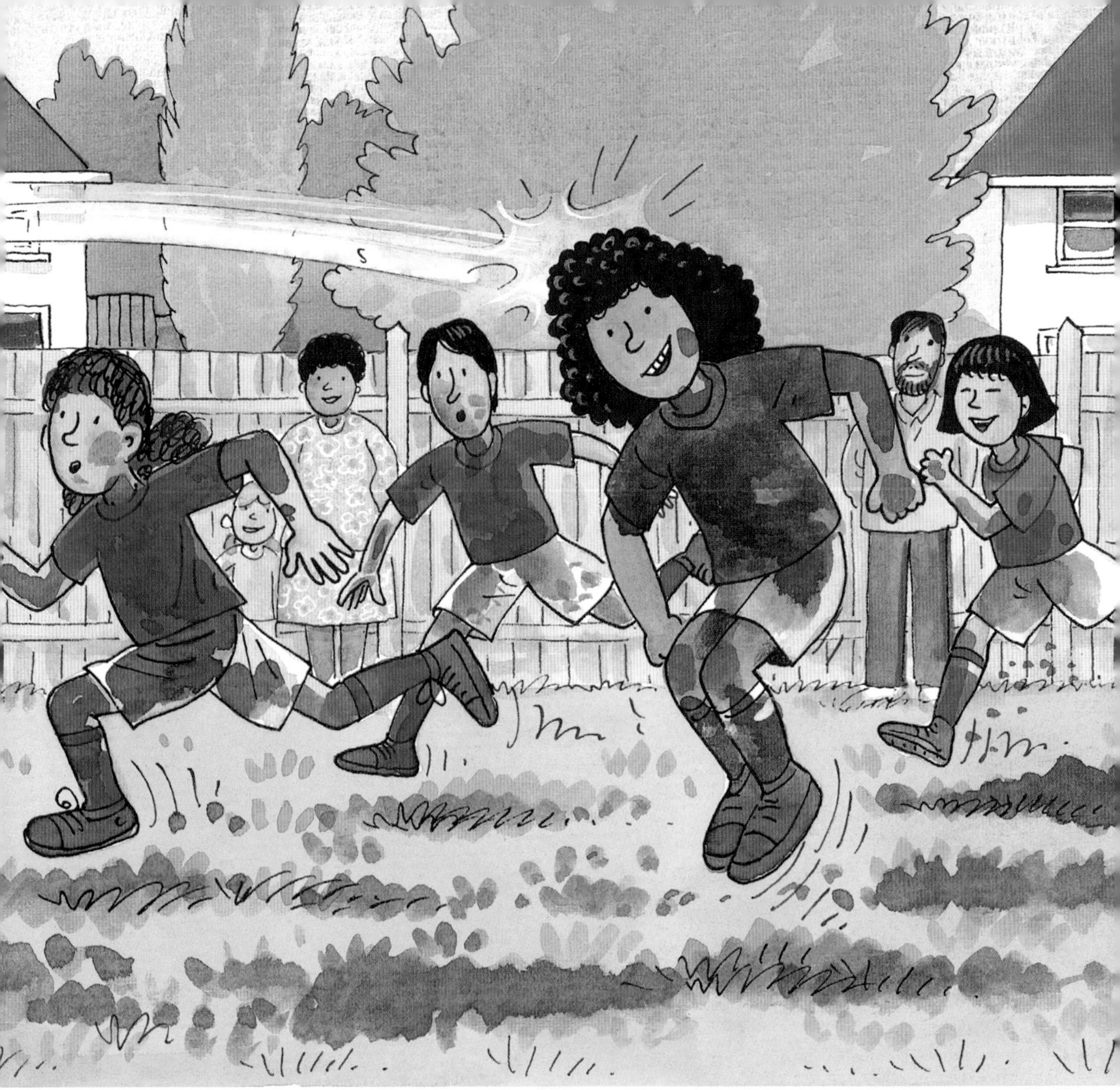

Who is in blue?

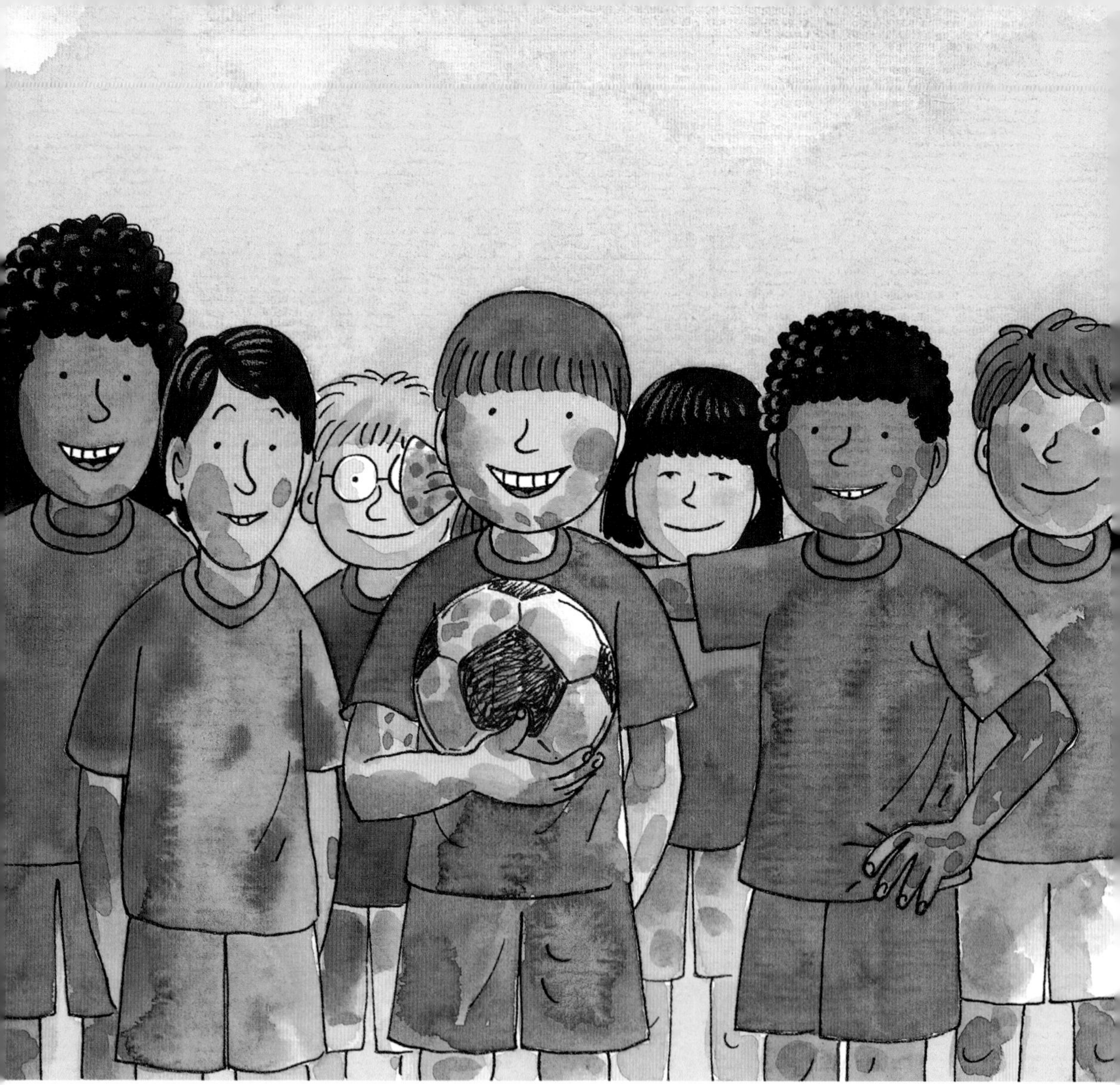

We are all muddy.